The Semi-Finals

Finally the office door opened and three men with clip-boards in their hands and whistles around their necks hustled out.

I felt a huge blob forming in my throat. This is it, I thought. Make it or break it.

"POP!" Bobby's gum was all over her lips. She casually peeled it off and resumed chewing.

I listened to the names being read off, and suddenly I heard my own name. "Leslie Crane!" Me! I made it to the finals! I was so excited I felt as if my bones had frozen.

And then—"Robinette Lorimer." Robinette! I looked at Bobby. She just grinned at me and blew another big bubble.

"POP!"

Books by Alison Jackson

My Brother the Star

Available from MINSTREL Books

MY BROTHER THE Star

Alison Jackson

illustrated by
Diane Dawson Hearn

A MINSTREL® BOOK

PUBLISHED BY POCKET BOOKS

New York   London   Toronto   Sydney   Tokyo   Singapore

To Mary and Steve,
because without their help
I never could have written this book.

A Minstrel Book published by
POCKET BOOKS, a division of Simon & Schuster Inc.
1230 Avenue of the Americas, New York, NY 10020

ISBN: 0-671-72863-6

First Minstrel Books printing May 1992

10 9 8 7 6 5 4 3 2 1

A MINSTREL BOOK and colophon are registered trademarks
of Simon & Schuster Inc.

Cover art by Daniel Horne

Printed in the U.S.A.

Chapter One

"Hey, let's face it," I complained, grabbing two cookies and glaring at the familiar face on my TV set. "My little brother IS cute."

"True," replied my best friend, Mike. He calmly swallowed one of his cookies in a single bite.

"And I'm a geek!" I added gloomily.

Mike just looked at me and laughed. "True," he said again.

I scowled back at him, saying nothing. My brother had that pudgy, round kind of face that made total strangers come up and pinch his cheeks. And his perfect blond curls and aqua blue eyes always started a commotion in the check-out line at the supermarket.

But enough was enough! If seeing my brother

at home every day didn't convince me that I was an ugly, skinny nobody, then staring at his face on the TV screen every Saturday morning certainly accomplished the same thing—instant depression!

And that's not even the worst of it. My name is Leslie Crane. And I'm a boy. Can you believe that? My mom says she named me after an old-time actor named Leslie Howard, but try to explain that to the thirty other kids in my fifth-grade class! She says that this *man* named Leslie played the part of a *man* named Ashley in *Gone With the Wind.*

Now, COME ON! Who is she trying to kid? There are two girls named Ashley in my classroom (and none named Leslie, thank goodness). But I have yet to meet any boy whose name even comes close to Ashley!

My little brother Cameron was also named after an actor. Someone called Cameron Mitchell. That's okay, I guess. As far as I have been able to tell, that name can go both ways. Besides, Cameron is an actor—sort of. He's been in a few magazine advertisements for some little toddler jeans, but his real thing is television commercials. In the past year, he's been in at least six or seven of them.

Now, am I jealous?

2

You bet I am! Just the sight of my brother chewing on a fruit roll-up bar makes my mouth fill up with spit. I start gagging before the roll-em-up song is even finished!

And I can't stand to look at a bowl of Yum-Yum Instant Oatmeal anymore. Because all I see is Cam on TV, shoving a spoonful of that gray lumpy stuff into his mouth and then smiling, with the oatmeal all stuck to his gums.

Cameron is cute and little and blond. I, on the other hand, am tall and skinny as a mop handle, with straight sandy-brown hair and eyes that are a color so dull there isn't even a name for it. My nose and teeth are too big for my face, and my feet are so huge that Cameron uses one of my old high tops as a submarine in the bathtub.

"I bet if I ran around the block naked, my mom wouldn't even notice," I sighed, while Mike nodded sympathetically. "Everything is always Cam, Cam, Cam."

As you can probably guess, I was a disappointment to my mother. Even from the beginning, Mom wanted to have a star in the family. She entered my picture in hundreds of baby photo contests, confident that my face had "character." But the answer was always the same: "N-O."

And even then my name was a curse. "Leslie appears to be an interesting child" one letter

3

said, "but she lacks the new 'look' that we are currently searching for." SHE!!!! See what I mean about my name? "Leslie Crane" sounds like some singing lady sprawled on top of a piano in a black slinky dress.

"You shouldn't worry so much about Cam being famous," Mike said with a shrug. "When he gets bigger he'll be out of work—pronto."

"Huh?"

"Smaller kids make the toys look bigger," Mike assured me as we lined up my slime men across the carpet in the den. "Besides, Cam'll start losing his teeth pretty soon, and then everyone will be able to see he's not in preschool."

"Yeah!" I answered, brightening a little. "When that first Oshkosh button pops, Cam will be a has-been!" And I'll be able to eat oatmeal again, I thought happily to myself.

Not that I didn't have a little bit of star quality too. You see, I was good at basketball and everyone knew it. There was nothing I loved more than shooting hoops all day. If I went for a jump shot, no one could touch me. And on a good day I could usually sink the ball from just about anywhere on the court. When we chose up teams after school, I was always the first one picked.

So I really was a star too, in a way. Only my parents didn't know it yet. I just had to find a way to show everyone that I could be as famous as my little brother—but in a different way.

At that very moment, the star himself walked into the den, sucking on a cherry Popsicle. Big red blobs of sticky goo were dripping from Cam's wrist onto the carpet.

"You can't eat that in here," I snapped at him. "If Mom sees you, you're gonna be dog meat."

Mike and I continued to line up our figures. Cam just slurped loudly. But I could tell he was itching to get his hands on those slime men. Oh, he didn't say anything. He just sat there and watched us. And waited. He knew that eventually either Mike or I would get up to go to the bathroom or something, so he just hovered.

It made me nervous. So I looked up at the television and yelled, "Hey, Cam! One of your commercials is on TV!"

Cam whipped his head around just in time to see a big brown dog lap up the remains of his food and then lick his slobbery chops.

"Liar!" Cam shouted at me. "I'm telling!"

"Don't you dare, or I'll tell Mom what you flushed down the toilet last night!"

"I'll tell first!"

"Fine." I carefully placed the slimy creatures back in my cigar box.

But before I could close the lid, Cam dropped

his Popsicle, grabbed one of the men, and began chewing on his head.

"Give him back!" I screamed at Cam.

"No," he answered, the two little legs sticking out of his mouth. By now the Popsicle was lying in a puddle on the coffee table.

"Mo-om!" I yelled, running into the kitchen. "Cam took one of my slime men and I told him to give it back, but he won't."

"Les, can't I trust you to watch Cam for even a few minutes without you picking on him?"

I gazed stupidly at her and blinked a few times.

"Now, I have to go to the store and buy another pound of hamburger for dinner tonight. Will you and Mike just try to include Cam in your fun for once? Please?"

I was unable to utter a word. Cam was always the good guy. I was pond scum.

With a huge sigh, I walked back to the den. Cam was forever trying to butt in when Mike and I were doing something fun together. Sometimes he just followed us around the house like a third shadow or something. Whenever he tagged along like that, I called him a first-stage nuisance.

Actually, I could put up with his shadow routine a lot easier than I could sit at the dinner table, watching him pop green peas into his mouth—one by one—while he chewed VERY

6

slowly. I mean, having him follow us was irritating, but it was not a cause for immediate death.

But if I walked into my room and found something like my science project painted all over with red lipstick squiggles, then I knew that Cam had advanced to a second-stage nuisance.

Now, a third-stage nuisance was the worst! When Cameron got to that stage, he would strut through the living room like some poodle in a dog show. At this point he had a real nose problem, and I needed to put him in his place. And it usually happened shortly after one of his commercials appeared on television.

It was bad enough when I had to look at Cam on the TV screen, but things got really uncomfortable when other people began to recognize my brother on television too.

In his latest commercial, he licked his upper lip (which was covered with some kind of runny chocolate glop) and said, "Mmmmmm. Yummy!" Then he rolled his eyes up into the top of his head. I have no idea where he learned to do that.

But when that ad came on halfway through "The Magical World of Disney" on Sunday night, I knew I was going to be dead meat on Monday morning.

Chapter Two

Sure enough, when I walked into class, Kevin Baker greeted me with "Mmmmmm. Yummy!" Then he licked his lips and rolled his eyes just like Cam.

I groaned and sat down.

"It's Leslie Crane—BROTHER of the star!" Kevin went on. His fat cheeks were bright pink from the enjoyment of torturing me. By this time most of the class was enjoying his performance too. The tops of my ears were burning. I just stared at my shoelaces.

Luckily, Mrs. Balcourt walked in at precisely that moment. Kevin rolled his eyes one more time and rubbed his tummy.

But the commercial that really cracked them all

up appeared on TV two weeks later. It was one in which Cam squeaked, "I want to be healthy and strong like my big brother," while he crunched away on some kind of breakfast cereal. Then the camera backed up to show his brother—easily a first-draft choice for the Rams.

The day after that one came on the air, Kevin Baker plopped an entire box (empty, of course) of Wheat Tootles on my desk. "Hey, Ichabod, you better eat these so that you can be healthy and strong like your LITTLE brother!" he snickered. I hugged my skinny arms across my chest and glared at him.

Ichabod! With my height and a last name like Crane, a lot of kids at school called me Ichabod. You know—like Ichabod Crane, the tall skinny guy that got chased out of Sleepy Hollow by the headless horseman?

"Come on, Kevin. Leave him alone." It was Mike, sticking up for me, as usual. He picked up the empty box and handed it back to Kevin. "It looks like you already ate them all anyway."

Kevin just laughed and imitated the now-famous Cameron eye roll, but he did sit down.

"You all right, Les?" whispered Mike, as he took his seat.

"Yeah. I guess."

This was all too humiliating. My mom had videotaped the commercial last night, and I must have watched Cam eating breakfast with that hulk twenty-five times. Now this!

Of course, I avoided Cam's taping sessions like the plague, even though Mike was always asking me what shooting a commercial was really like. No way was I going to sit and watch my brother being the center of attention—and getting paid for it! I saw enough of his face at home. And I wasn't about to give him the satisfaction.

"Every time I turn the set on, there's Cam's face staring at me," I told Mike as we walked home from school. By this time Cam had starred in seven different commercials, and I had seen each one of them at least five times.

"Sometimes he's on two different channels at once! It's like being in 'The Twilight Zone.'"

"Yeah. I guess I'd be pretty jealous too," Mike answered.

"JEALOUS! Who, me???"

Mike hesitated. "Well . . . angry," he said finally.

"Just annoyed," I replied. "But Cam's coming real close to being a third-stage nuisance."

I didn't tell Mike that I really wanted to be famous too. He would have laughed his head off.

11

When the two of us got home, Cam was chasing Thai—our Siamese cat—into the dark slanty place under the stairs. Poor Thai was still suffering from shell shock because Cam had drenched him last night with his new water gun.

Just then my mother charged out of the den with her purse slung over one shoulder. A sure sign of trouble.

"Could you please watch Cam for an hour or so?" Mom asked me breathlessly. "I have to run into L.A. and sign a release form for his next commercial. Oh, hi, Mike! There are some cookies in the kitchen, you two."

And she was gone.

Mike and I looked at each other, and then we started laughing. He was used to exits like this at my house. We decided to sample the cookies before going outside to practice some shots.

As soon as Cam discovered that he was in the house with just Mike and me, he yelled, "Ride 'em, horsey!" and jumped right at Thai. The cat just rolled over and poked his claws through my brother's jeans until Cam started squealing like a stuck pig.

I wrenched the two of them apart, and Thai bolted out of the house through his kitty door. Then I sat Cam in a chair and scolded him.

"I'll give you sixty seconds to behave yourself," I said.

"You turd-head, you!" he yelled back at me.

"You be good, or I'll never let you stay up past ten o'clock again as long as you live on this planet."

He sat in silence. Finally he sniffled and put on his angelic TV face. "I promise to be good, Les," he said. I just gave Mike a doubtful look over Cam's head.

"Man!" Mike exclaimed. "If he pounds on the cat like that, what does he do to your hamster?"

"NOTHING!" I said. Cameron opened his mouth but then decided to shut it again.

"Or else!" I added. Max, my pet hamster, was thoroughly off limits, and Cam knew it.

When Mom came home, I asked if Mike and I could walk to the 7-Eleven to play Space Invaders. She sighed and pulled out her change purse. "Just be back in time to help set the table for dinner," she reminded me.

"No fair!" piped in Cameron. (Where had he been hiding?) "What about me?"

Mom handed him fifty cents. "You can go too, Cam," she said.

"But Mo-om." I was whining, and I knew it.

"It won't hurt you to just take him two blocks,"

Mom answered. When she turned her back, Cam stuck out his tongue at me.

Of course, before Mike and I even finished two games of Space Invaders, Cam wanted to go home. "I'm hungry!" he cried in that high squeaky voice of his that sounded like Mickey Mouse.

"If you hadn't spent your fifty cents on comic books, you could have gotten something to eat," I huffed, thoroughly disgusted.

A woman walked by with a shopping basket and stopped in front of Cam. She was studying his face, and I just knew she would recognize him in another minute or two.

"What a beautiful child!" she exclaimed. Cam cheered up miraculously.

"I'm sure I know you," she continued. "What's your name, little girl?"

Cam was so surprised at being mistaken for a girl that he didn't answer her. Of course, with a name like Leslie I was used to that sort of thing, so I did.

"That's Cam," I announced, in my most polite, out-in-public voice. Then, realizing that the woman still thought Cam was a girl, I added, "He's a boy."

"Oh." She paused. "What is your name?"

"Leslie," I replied. "And I'm a son of a gun." I

14

could have said something much worse, but I knew Cam would tell on me.

It was enough. The woman turned and huffed out of the store.

The three of us watched as she pushed her way through the double doors and climbed into a blue station wagon.

"Hey, Les! That lady said I'm beautiful."

"Sooooo?"

"So, that means you're uglier than DIRT!"

See what I mean? A third-stage nuisance, for sure.

Chapter Three

During math the next morning, Melissa Harding entered the room and walked up to Mrs. Balcourt with a folded note. She was always running errands for the principal or the school nurse, so no one paid much attention to her. But this time Melissa placed her message importantly on the teacher's desk and then headed back down MY aisle, her eyes squinting directly at me.

"Ooooooh . . . you're in troooooouuuuuble!" she whispered.

"Les and Mike," Mrs. Balcourt began, after reading the note carefully. "You are both wanted in the vice-principal's office. Immediately."

Neither one of us had ever spoken to Mr. Eastwood in person before! Not outside of open house, anyway. I glanced over at Kevin Baker, who was grinning at me like a cat. Kevin was a frequent visitor to the vice-principal's office.

Mike and I walked down the hall in silence, but I raised one eyebrow at him, kind of like sign language for "What in the world did we do?" He just shrugged.

By the time we reached Mr. Eastwood's office, I had already decided that it must be Cam who was in trouble. Maybe he caused his first-grade teacher to have a nervous breakdown and we were expected to walk him home from school.

But when Mike and I shuffled inside to take a seat, Cam was nowhere in sight. I sat on the edge of the chair and stuck my legs way out. If I stretched real hard, I could almost touch the wastebasket with the toes of my shoes.

"Hello, boys," Mr. Eastwood greeted us. He was smiling, which was a good sign, I guess. "How are you?"

"Fine," I answered.

"Yeah," replied Mike, sitting up very straight. "I mean, I'm fine too, . . . sir."

"The reason I called you in is because the county school system is sponsoring its annual sports camp this summer, and I think you two have a good chance of making the basketball team. I'd like to see you representing Riverdale Elementary."

As I let this sink in, a warm tingle ran up my arm and stopped at my throat. I wanted to yell and jump up in the air, but I sat very still. There had to be a catch.

"The camp is really for junior high and high school students, but exceptional sixth graders are encouraged to apply."

"We're only in fifth grade," Mike blurted out. I could have shot him.

"After this summer you will be entering the sixth grade," Mr. Eastwood answered slowly, as if Mike were a moron.

"Oh. Yeah."

"The tryouts will be on May 14. That's in six weeks. It will be an elimination tournament among all the schools in Riverdale. Then the county finals will be held three weeks after that. Are you interested?"

"Yes!" we both shouted. Then we grinned at each other.

"Fine. Here are the applications. Take them home and have your parents sign them." He handed the two sheets of paper to us and stood there, waiting for us to leave. I guess he was a pretty busy man.

I folded up the application and slid it into my pocket. Then Mike and I walked back down the hall without saying a word. Recess had already started, but we didn't even notice. Both of us were sort of in a daze.

Suddenly we started running side by side, pretending that we were dribbling a ball down center court.

"Magic Mike Lucas breaks to the middle and passes off to Kareem Crane!" Mike shouted, springing up on his toes.

The invisible ball left my fingertips with a perfect backspin and snapped into our imaginary net. I spun around like a top. "Two points for Crane!" I shouted. Then we both collapsed in front of the girls' bathroom, laughing hysterically.

Just then, Melissa Harding opened the door and leaned over our sprawled bodies, her face all crinkled up like a raisin.

"If you are trying to peek under the door, I think that is TOTALLY disgusting!" she said, and edged her way around us, heading toward the playground.

We couldn't help it. We cracked up again. And we didn't stop laughing until the bell rang.

That night I told Mom and Dad about the tryouts. I was so excited that I could hardly eat dinner.

"Well, Les," my dad replied, grinning at me, "I couldn't be more proud of you." Dad had played a little basketball in college himself.

Even Mom was excited, although sports was not exactly her interest. "You mean that you and Mike were actually called into the principal's office? Just the two of you?"

"Well . . . the vice-principal's office," I mumbled.

Cam broke in. "I went to the principal's office once to get an excuse form for one of my commercials."

"Then I guess Les and Mike will need some pointers before the big day," Dad said. "How about if I—"

"Could you pass the butter?" Cam interrupted.

Mom was studying me carefully. "How old did you say these boys are?"

"Twelve to eighteen," I answered proudly. "But I won't—"

"Could you pass the milk?" Cam asked. No one did.

"I don't know. . . ." muttered my mother. "Sending a fifth grader in with all those high school boys . . ."

"I'll be a SIXTH grader, Mom. Besides, the rules said the camp will be divided into different probably never even lay eyes on a high school kid."

"But still," my mom persisted, "basketball is a contact sport, and some of those eighth graders are pretty big boys."

"Yeah," Cameron piped in again. "Those big fat guys will stomp right on Leslie's head!"

I couldn't believe this was happening to me! Mom and Cam were going to ruin my life right here at the dinner table.

Then Dad cleared his throat and started to speak slowly. "Well, I don't know, Jan. Les is a pretty good ballplayer. And he could probably use some tougher competition. I think he needs to go to that sports camp this summer."

Mom didn't answer right away, and I tried to hold back a grin. Even Cam didn't have anything to say. I turned my head to make a face at him, but all I saw was his empty chair.

Suddenly we all heard a scream, and each one of us took off in a different direction. I was the one who discovered my brother. He was lying in our driveway under the basketball hoop. Next to him was an overturned lawn chair.

Cam was as white as the chalk Mrs. Balcourt used to demonstrate our math problems. When I stooped down, his face sort of squeezed together, tears streaming down both sides and into his ears.

"My arm," he hollered. "It really HURTS!" Then he screamed out in pain again.

"Don't move," I told him. "I'll get Mom and Dad." I started to turn away when I saw that my basketball had rolled across the driveway and was lying in Mom's begonias. I looked back at Cam. His bottom lip was quivering up and down.

"What in the heck were you doing anyway?"

"Trying to shoot a basket," he said. "Like you." Then Cam started yelling again, this time for Mom and Dad.

By now they had found the two of us, and my mother shrieked when she got one look at Cam.

"Get him in the car," she ordered. "We're going to the emergency room."

Chapter Four

By the time we got home from the hospital, it was after ten o'clock. Cam's arm was in a cast, and he was pretty sleepy. After Mom put him to bed, she sat down with me at the kitchen table.

"Now, Les. I want you to be very considerate of Cam while his arm is in that cast," she told me. Mom ALWAYS wanted me to be very considerate of Cam.

"How long will that be?" I asked, sulking a little.

"About six weeks."

Six weeks. That was when the first tryouts for the county basketball camp were scheduled, but I was sure Mom had forgotten all about the tryouts now. For the next six weeks my brother was going to be the center of attention. He had done it to me again.

Cam slept off and on for about two days, but since I shared a room with him, I was the one who got to listen to him whine whenever he was up.

On Thursday he woke me in the middle of the night to complain about his cast itching.

"It's your arm that itches, Cam," I grumbled. "Not the cast. Now go back to sleep."

He was quiet for about one minute. Then he started in again.

"Will you sign it first?"

"Sign what?" I asked, half asleep.

"My cast."

I crawled out of bed and turned on the light. Then I took one of his Magic Markers and wrote, *Tough break. Ha! Ha!—Les.*

Cam studied it for a moment, his forehead wrinkled up in concentration. "You know I can't read cursive yet. I'm only in the first grade! What does it say?"

I told him. His face sagged.

"What's the matter *now*?" I was cold, standing there outside of the covers, and my own bed on the other side of the room sure looked cozy to me right now.

25

"I wanted you to sign it *Kareem*," Cam pouted.

Boy! I crossed out *Les* and scribbled *Kareem*. He seemed happy now.

"Let's use my Play-Doh," he suggested. I hate that stuff because Cam drops it and it hardens into little rocks right on the rug. Then my mom says I have to clean it up because I'm old enough to know better. That's a fight I can never win.

"No way," I said, starting to climb back into bed.

"But you make the best Play-Doh dinosaurs. Can't you show me how to do a stegosaurus?"

I looked at my brother sitting up in bed. He was cradling his cast in the other arm and reading my signature on the white plaster, his lips curved up in a smile.

Oh, well. Maybe I could just help him this once, I thought to myself. After all, molding Play-Doh with one hand was probably pretty tough.

I pulled on a sweat shirt and sat down on the bed next to him. We made some green dinosaurs and molded space creatures out of the blue Play-Doh.

I put my creature down and studied the top of Cam's head. There was still one thing I had to know.

"Hey, Cam?" I asked. "Did you really need that chair?"

Cam looked up at me. "How else could I reach the basket, dumb-head?"

I started to tell him that I couldn't reach the basket either, but right about then Cam's eyelids began to close.

"Let's go to bed, champ," I said, and I tucked him in under his Batman sheets.

I turned out the light and snuggled under my own covers. Then something very important struck me.

"Cam?" I said, sitting straight up in bed.

"Mmmm?"

"If your arm is broken, you're sort of out of the commercial business for a while, aren't you—unless they do one about broken bones."

"Yeah. I sure am." His muffled reply was so soft that I could have been hearing things. Was I imagining it, or did that little voice sound happy?

It didn't take me long to stop feeling sorry for my brother. Once his arm finally stopped hurting, he milked this thing for all he could get! I began to understand why Cam was so delighted with his new situation. After all, filming commercials was probably pretty hard work compared with being pampered while he sat around all day with his arm in a sling.

"How come Cam can't even help with the dinner dishes?" I complained one night. I figured he could at least manage to rinse a plate with one hand.

"Because he doesn't know how," Mom answered. I thought that was pretty silly, because who needed a vocational training course to scrape meat loaf off a plate?

Then my mom added, "He'll just clutter up the kitchen."

"Why don't you let Cam at least help me rinse?" I mumbled.

"No, no, no. His cast will get all wet."

"Well, he didn't break his leg. He could put some of the salad plates away."

Mom gave me a look.

"It's not MY fault he broke his arm." Now I was treading on thin ice. I mean, Cam wouldn't have been trying to shoot baskets in the first place if I hadn't been carrying on about the try-outs that night. I considered myself lucky to even be trying out for basketball camp at all.

After Mom left, I finished the dishes in stony silence. By bedtime I had almost convinced myself that Cam's arm wasn't really even broken. He had probably charmed the doctor into putting a cast on him just so that he could torment me.

I lay in bed and listened to Cam thrashing around, trying to get the cast situated just right.

28

Every once in a while he'd make a little snort with his nose.

"Nyaw! Nyaw! Nyaw!"

"Mom!" I yelled, jumping out of bed and racing down the hall. "He's snorting again. I can't sleep!"

Mom walked back to my room with me, her arm around my shoulder. "Please stop snorting, Cam," she said to him. And she went back to bed.

Just like that. I'm not kidding! She really believed that Cam would stop snorting because she asked him to!

But did Mom even stick around? No. That was my job. To put up with a snorting little brother in the middle of the night. In the dark.

"Nyaw! Nyaw! Nyaw!" Cam started snorting and wiggling around again as soon as she was gone. That kid could even bug me in his sleep.

I swore—again—that when I grew up I would never EVER EVER make my kids share a room. Even if one of them had to sleep in the bathtub!

Whenever we got a chance, Mike and I played a little one-on-one. I had been shooting hoops with him for so many years that it seemed as if we actually lived on a basketball court. I always felt more comfortable when I had a ball in the palm of my hand. Like it belonged there or something.

But neither of us had ever played a game against a bunch of older guys before, and we were both pretty jittery. Two days before the try-outs Mike showed up with a basketball under his arm, ready to shoot some serious baskets.

He did a couple of head fakes to the right and then pivoted, spinning around to the left. But I was all over him and he got rattled. Mike tried to work the ball in, but then he double dribbled, so I yelled at him to stop.

He suddenly turned around and looked at me, frowning. "Hey, Les. What if one of us makes it and the other one doesn't?" he asked, spinning the ball on the tip of his index finger.

I hadn't thought of that. But it sure looked as if Mike had. A lot. I hoped he wasn't going to ask me to drop out if I was picked to go to camp without him. I mean, he was my best friend and all, but I would even have taken Cam with me if it meant I could play ball for three solid weeks!

Mike sort of sighed and then smiled, tossing the ball to me. "I know you're a lot better than I am, Les," he said quietly.

How do you tell someone he's just about the best friend anybody ever had? I only shrugged, gazing down at the pavement. Then I dribbled the ball a few times.

"Oh, I don't know," I muttered. "It sure would be a lot more fun if both of us could go."

"Yeah," he answered.

We started shooting baskets again.

Just then, Cam ran out of the house with his friend Jerome. Unfortunately, now that Cam was temporarily unemployed, he was home every afternoon with me.

"Les! Come quick!" Cam cried. "I think your hamster must be sick or something!"

I threw the ball down and raced upstairs to our room. My hamster was lying on his side in the bottom of the cage, barely breathing. Max always slept on his stomach, so I knew right away that something was wrong.

"What happened?" I shouted at Cam and Jerome. "Did you two do something to him?"

Their eyes bugged out, and Jerome backed up a few steps.

"No," they both replied.

"Did you take Max out of the cage?" Cam knew that was forbidden unless I was in the room with him.

"No. Uh-unh. No way."

I opened the cage and lifted Max out in the

31

palm of my hand. He was still lying on his side, not moving, but he might have just been paralyzed with fright. I mean, Max was a great hamster and all, but he got a little paranoid around Cam sometimes, especially since my brother liked to stick his finger in the cage and throw hardened Play-Doh pellets into his drinking water.

"I just don't understand it," I said to Mike. "Max was fine this morning." I turned back to Cam and Jerome.

"Are you absolutely SURE you didn't take Max out of his cage?"

"Well, we MIGHT have taken him out, but only for a minute or so," Cam finally said.

"But what did you do with him?" I screamed.

Then I noticed Max's exercise ball on the floor over near the bookcase. It was a clear plastic ball that came apart around the middle, so that Max could play in it and make the ball roll around on the floor just by running inside. I put him in the ball sometimes so that he could jog around the room without running away from me or trying to hide somewhere.

"Did you put this hamster in the exercise ball?" I asked Cam, totally furious.

"No. No way!" said Cameron.

"Did you take the ball out of the cage?"

"No. Un-unh."

"Then how did it get over there? You know that ball is always kept inside Max's cage!"

Cameron looked over at the ball on the floor and saw that there was no way out of this one.

"Well, we MIGHT have taken the ball out—but just for a minute."

"Did you roll Max on the floor in the ball?"

"No." Cam shook his head firmly back and forth.

"Did you put Max into the ball at all?"

"Well, we MIGHT have put Max in there, but just for a minute."

I was afraid to find out where all of this might be leading, but I was at least relieved to see that Max was beginning to wiggle in the palm of my hand. Mike started to chuckle—he couldn't help it—and I glared at him.

"Did you roll the ball on the floor at all?" I asked Cam again.

"No. Uh-unh."

"Did you move it in any way?"

Cam looked at Jerome and shrugged. "Yes," he admitted.

"Well, if you didn't roll it, what did you DO with it?"

"Ummm, we MIGHT have thrown it back and forth, just once or twice."

"What?" I shrieked. "You played catch? With Max inside?"

By this time Jerome was crying and Cam was close to it.

"Get out!" I screamed at both of them. "Before I start playing catch with your heads!"

They scurried out the door, and I gently placed Max back into the cage. He was moving now, and his eyes were open. He stood up on his legs and blinked slowly. Then he turned his back on me and went to the bathroom on a little corner of shredded newspaper. Well, it looked as if he might survive this trauma after all.

Mike had collapsed on the floor, laughing. Pretty soon even I had to laugh. Then I rolled back and forth on the floor with him, holding my stomach because it hurt so much.

"Man!" I finally said. "I sure can't wait until Cam gets that cast off."

"I bet Max can't either!" Mike hollered, starting to giggle all over again. And we rolled on the floor some more.

Chapter Five

On the morning of the basketball tryouts I woke up before anyone else. It was still dark outside. I looked around the room, examining the gray shadows of all my familiar belongings. Even in the darkness, I could pick out each item from memory: my globe of the earth, the model I made of a California mission last year, my poster that said "I Got Slimed!"

This afternoon I will be looking at all of these same things again, I thought. Only it will be different. I'll either be very happy—or wishing I was dead.

I glanced over at my brother and noticed that he had kicked off all his covers, so I crept quietly to his bed and leaned over to pull them up.

Cam's eyes opened just below my own, and he

nearly jumped out of his skin. "What're YOU looking at?" he demanded.

"Nothing."

"What do you mean, nothing? You can't look at nothing. You're looking at me!"

"Okay. I'm looking at you now. But I WAS looking at all my stuff."

"Your stuff? Why?"

"Because this is kind of a big day for me. The tryouts—remember?"

"Oh."

"I'm really nervous. Don't you ever feel nervous before you film a TV commercial?" I asked him, actually kind of curious. We never talked much about his commercials because I always pretended that I just didn't care.

Cam had confessed to me once that he hated Yum-Yum Instant Oatmeal, but he usually didn't discuss his TV commercials unless Mom was around to make a big fuss over him.

"No," he mumbled, sitting up in his bed. "They're dumb."

"Huh?" I leaned forward to hear more. This was juicy.

"I use these dumb little toys made for four-year-olds," Cam said. He picked up one of the Play-Doh dinosaurs from his bedside table. One of its feet fell off onto his lap. "And I have to wear baby clothes and say baby things like 'Mmmmmm. Yummy!' It's just . . . dumb."

Now I knew why Cam was enjoying his broken arm so much. It wasn't only the attention. It was because for a while he was a normal kid who could come home from school and watch a little TV and maybe even have a friend over to play (or bother my hamster).

"Can't you tell Mom that?" I asked, but I knew it would be impossible the minute I said it. Mom had spent the last ten years trying to get one of us on television. And now that my brother was a success, Mom was blazing a path clear to Hollywood.

Cam just gave me a look with those watery blue eyes. He was normally a pretty gutsy kid, but even Attila the Hun couldn't have taken on my mother when she got into one of her TV frenzies! I wouldn't have had the nerve to do it either.

I actually felt sorry for this kid. Sitting down on the edge of his bed, I signaled for Cam to scoot over next to me. Then I sort of patted him on the top of the leg, but I didn't say anything.

"Can you maybe show me how to shoot baskets sometime?" asked Cam. He was trying to stick the dinosaur foot back on. "After my cast is off, I mean?"

"Sure. Maybe we can put up a shorter hoop for you. So you don't have to go climbing on any more chairs."

Cam smiled at me. "Let's play Legos!" he said.

"Well . . . okay."

It was still early, but we pulled out the Legos and built an entire model of Disneyland, complete with Adventureland and Frontierland. It took almost two hours. And it sure helped me, because I didn't think about the tryouts once until Mom called us downstairs for breakfast.

When the whistle blew, I already knew who had fouled. Leslie Crane . . . again. I just couldn't help it. This little runty kid with short, curly hair kept darting in and out, and I always seemed to land right on top of him whenever I was in control of the ball. His man-to-man defense was incredible.

We were each being called in to play at five-minute intervals, and I wondered how the other players sitting in the bleachers would do against this short kid. Maybe I could ask one of them.

Not that any of these guys would tell me anyway. They were all in junior high school, and I was just a crummy fifth grader. Besides, some of them had already gone through this last year. And most of them had probably played on these bigger courts before and figured they were shoo-ins.

Our team called a time-out, and we met on the bench.

"Crane, you've got to watch out for Bobby," said Tim Lorimer. Tim was an eighth grader who had already attended the sports camp last summer. He was tall and dark—and always very cool.

"Who?" I asked Tim, blinking up at him.

"The munchkin."

"Oh. Yeah." I would have to start looking down more, instead of up at the hoop.

I noticed one guy next to me slurping loudly on an orange. The juice was dribbling down his chin and into the top of his tank shirt. Just watching it made the sides of my mouth pucker up, aching for a taste.

"Where can I get some oranges?" I asked him, licking my dry lips.

He looked blankly at me and set the orange rind down on the bench between us. "From a tree," he said.

See what I mean? I couldn't count on a whole lot of help from these guys.

"Hey," interrupted one of the other bigger players, "did any of you guys smell strawberries when you were out there?"

Come to think of it, I had caught a whiff of strawberries every now and then.

"Peeeee Uuuuuuu. I sure did!" yelled Tim, rushing back out to the court. "It was probably Bobby!" Everyone laughed—except for me. I didn't get it. What did that little guy have to do with strawberries?

I played better during the second half, but I still had trouble shooting whenever the munchkin was around. He sure was quick, although he wasn't too good at making steals. I did get free one time, and I worked myself into the corner of the court. I watched Tim make a pass to the center, who passed off to me. Without hesitating, I snapped the ball up in a perfect arch—BINGO—and I canned a clean shot, tying the game.

In the last five minutes I heard a familiar voice.

"Hey, Ichabod! Over here!" It was Mike, calling to me from across the court. I passed the ball to him and he took a wild shot from the perimeter, totally missing the backboard. Too bad. He should have taken more time to aim. Even the munchkin had been nowhere near him.

The last whistle blew, and the game was over. Tim Lorimer walked over to me and slapped me on the back.

"Great game, Ichabod," he said. Oh, jeez! Did he really think that was my name?

"Thanks," I said. Then Tim grinned at me and held out his hand. I shook it and suddenly felt as if I were ten feet tall. Tim Lorimer really thought I was good!

We all sat around waiting to hear the results. Everyone tried to act as if he didn't care, but each time the door to the office opened, we jerked our heads around in unison.

The runty kid started walking over to us, chewing on a huge wad of gum, and I had to try and keep from staring. Up closer, his face looked pretty young. How did he expect to compete with all of these junior high school guys?

"Hey, Ichabod! Nice game," he said, grinning at me.

Oh, no! The munchkin was talking to me! I turned to say something to Tim Lorimer, trying to pretend that Bobby hadn't spoken. After all, hadn't they all been making fun of him? I wanted to look cool, and this little runt was blowing my cover.

"Nice game," the kid repeated, a little louder this time. I turned—and was suddenly face to face with him.

"I'm talking to YOU, Crane!" Bobby said.

But I couldn't answer. I was staring right into a pair of big brown eyes with thick lashes. All

I could smell was the overwhelming odor of strawberries.

He was a she! I mean, the munchkin was a girl! But that wasn't all.

"I'm Bobby Lorimer," she said, holding out her hand.

Oh, great! Tim's sister!

"Is your name really Ichabod?" Bobby demanded, blowing a huge pink bubble and letting it pop all over her mouth and nose. Now the strawberry odor grew even stronger. It was the bubble gum. Gross!

"Uh—no," I answered slowly. "My name's Leslie. Leslie Crane."

"LESLIE!"

"Shhhhh!" I hissed.

"Sorry. But that name stinks! Someone might think you're a girl, for crying out loud!" Bobby tossed her head in disgust.

Yeah, I thought. And someone might think that YOU are a boy. But I didn't say it. I was about to tell her that the gum smelled pretty sickening when the office door opened and three men with clipboards in their hands and whistles around their necks hustled out.

We all quieted down and stared at them, silently praying.

"First of all," yelled the biggest one, "you were all great!" A few of us clapped our hands. "But we could only choose six people in each category."

I felt a huge blob forming in my throat. This is it, I thought. Make it or break it.

"POP!" Bobby's bubble gum was all over her lips. She casually peeled it off and resumed chewing. That smelly gum was about to make me throw up. Maybe that's what was stuck in my throat—barf! Now I didn't even dare to open my mouth.

I listened to the names being read off, and suddenly I heard my own name. "Leslie Crane!" Me! I made it to the finals. I was so excited that I felt as if all my bones had frozen. I couldn't move, and my face was tingling.

Then I heard the man yell out, "Tim Lorimer." Good, I thought. Somehow I just knew that Tim and I were going to be good buddies this summer.

And then—"Robinette Lorimer." Robinette!!!!! That wasn't such a hot name either. Who was she to tell me that my name stinks?

I looked at Bobby. She just grinned at me and blew another big bubble.

"POP!"

Chapter Six

Tim was suddenly slapping me on the back and Bobby was yelling her head off. I was pretty busy slapping and yelling too, so it took me a while to notice that Mike wasn't with our group anymore. He must have slipped away right after the announcements.

Then I saw him. He was sitting on the lower bleachers on the other side of the gym. And he looked like Mr. Agony: the skier who took down an entire fence every Saturday at the beginning of "Wide World of Sports." I was so excited when Tim pounded me on the back that I had completely forgotten about Mike.

Well, I felt like a pretty rotten person. I walked over to him, with my arms dangling at my sides.

What do you say to a guy who's just been beaten out by his best friend and a munchkin?

"Hi," I mumbled.

"Hi."

"Gosh. I'm sorry, Mike."

"It's no big deal." He rubbed the toe of his sneaker into the hardwood floor.

"Do you kind of hate me? Huh?"

"Yeah," Mike answered. "I do." His mouth looked straight and tight.

This isn't fair, I wanted to shout! How could I feel so happy for me and so rotten about Mike at the same time? It should have been him out there shooting hoops with me during the finals instead of some dumb girl!

Leslie Crane was going to be a star—and I couldn't even enjoy it.

I sat down next to Mike and stared out across the empty courts. Then I rubbed my sweaty palms across the front of my T-shirt.

"You wanna go get an ice cream cone?" I said after a while.

Mike looked up at me. "I don't have any money."

"I do."

"Okay."

After changing our clothes, we walked all the

way to Swensen's and never even talked about the tryouts or anything. I figured that Mike would mention it when he was ready. You just kind of know these things when you've been friends as long as we have.

We finished our double-decker chocolate cones, and then I walked Mike to the corner of his street.

"Hey, Les," he said, switching his gym bag over to the other shoulder, "that was really great for you. I mean, about the tryouts."

"Yeah. Well. I wish you could've made it too."

"Yeah. Well." He shrugged and smiled at me.

"See you tomorrow?" I asked.

"Sure."

I watched him shuffle off down the sidewalk and up to his house. As soon as I saw him go inside, I turned and ran the rest of the way home to tell my mom all about the tryouts.

Mom was getting dinner ready, and I yelled out my good news. "Hey, Mom! I made it into the finals!"

"Oh, Les!" she cried, running over to hug me. It was a little awkward because her head fit just under my nose, but it felt awfully good anyway. "I'm so proud of you! Should we call your father at the car lot?"

"No. Let's just wait until he gets home."

"Have some cookies to celebrate," she said, giving me another squeeze. Then she handed me four homemade cookies.

"Take two of these in to Cam while you're at it," she added.

Suddenly my excitement fizzled. I should have known HE would figure into this somehow.

Cam was in the den, his eyes glued to the television screen, watching "The Adventures of Gumby." I handed him the cookies and then glanced over at the TV.

Gumby and his friend Pokey were dressed in space suits. The green point on Gumby's head poked through the top of his space helmet. They were on their way to another planet or something.

I flopped myself down on the couch. "Can't you be a little more picky about what you watch?"

Cam continued to stare straight ahead, munching on Mom's cookies.

"This is dumb!" I said. "It takes days, or even months, to get to the nearest planet. Besides, why aren't Gumby and Pokey weightless? How can they breathe? And what about food? There are no animals or vegetables on any of the other planets in our solar system."

"Ha!" yelled Cam, but his eyes still remained

fixed on the TV. "That just shows what YOU know! Gumby's made out of clay, so he doesn't breathe or eat anyway!"

I realized that he had a point here. When the show was over, I picked myself up and went to the kitchen for a glass of water.

Cam followed me and sat down at the kitchen table.

"Cameron, your brother made the basketball team. Isn't that exciting?" Mom asked him.

"Just the first cut," I added quickly.

Cam didn't say anything at first, but his eyes squinted into tiny slits. "Well, I get my cast off on Monday," he replied. I knew that he was only trying to lure Mom away from his least favorite topic—me! But it sort of backfired on him.

Mom beamed at me. "Yes, isn't that great? I've had to turn down two commercials since that thing was put on, but now Cam can start working again." She turned back to the stove, and I studied Cam as he traced little circles on the tabletop. Over the weeks, his cast had gotten pretty dirty and gray around the edges where his fingers peeked out.

I remembered what Cam told me this morning—about the dumb commercials and the baby clothes he had to wear. Poor guy. I really felt sorry for him, even if he did terrorize the cat and snort in his sleep and turn my hamster into a neurotic.

"That's good news about your cast," I said to Cam. "Maybe we can shoot some baskets soon."

Cam looked up, smiling at me. And I thought that maybe I wasn't such a bad guy after all.

Chapter Seven

The next day was Sunday. Cam's cast would be coming off on Monday, and he was scheduled to film a new commercial on Wednesday afternoon. Mom sure hadn't wasted any time!

On Sunday night she made my brother try on a pair of red plaid Oshkosh overalls, to see if they would still fit for the commercial, but they didn't. Then she tried the little blue sailor suit. The shorts barely made it up over his butt.

Cam's face was looking pretty grim. I don't think he wanted to be caught dead in any of this stuff, but Mom always dressed him like a baby for television, because it made him look younger.

"What have you been eating the last six

weeks?" Mom exclaimed, close to tears. She was squeezing Cam into a pair of striped blue pants, trying to fasten the buttons around his waist.

One of the buttons snapped off and flew across the room. Thai shot under the bed after the button. Poor Max, now nicknamed Schizo Hamster, ran into the side of his cage and nearly died of a heart attack. He wouldn't go near the exercise ball anymore—and even the slightest noise would make him go to the bathroom instantly, no matter where he happened to be.

"This is terrible!" my mother shrieked. "What if Cam ends up to be—TALL?"

"There are worse things in life," I mumbled, but she didn't hear me. Besides, what did she expect? My dad was over six feet tall, and I had already reached five feet seven inches myself.

Mom ran to find a tape measure and then hurriedly knelt down to measure my brother.

"Oh, dear," she sighed. "He's grown three whole inches in just a month and a half. This is horrible."

Cam looked up at me, and a slow grin formed on his face. In the end, Mom finally had to settle on a pair of blue cords and a striped T-shirt, the clothes Cam probably would have picked anyway.

Later—in bed—I was almost asleep when I felt heavy breathing across my face. It was Cam, standing by my head and breathing through his mouth in the dark.

"Jeez, Cam!" I said. "I thought you were the abominable snowman, coming to eat my nose off."

Cam held up the cast and plopped it across my stomach. He had a serious look on his face.

"Can I ask you something, Les?"

"Mmmmm?"

"I'm scared. What if my arm didn't grow in there?" he whispered urgently.

I decided that maybe I had just heard him wrong. "Didn't grow what?" I asked.

"At all."

I stopped to think about that. "Why wouldn't it?"

"Well, I grew three inches, but the cast didn't—and my arm was stuck in there."

"For Pete's sake, Cam," I hissed loudly, "I wouldn't worry about that! Your arm'll probably fall off onto the floor the minute the doctor yanks the cast off."

Cam started to cry, and I felt like Mr. Rotten.

"I was only kidding, Cam," I said more gently. Then I patted the pillow beside my head. "Come on, sport," I said. "Crawl in with me." So he did.

I wrapped one arm around him and closed my eyes.

"Les?" Cam whispered, as I was almost asleep.

"Huh?" I grunted.

"Can you maybe come with Mom and me on Wednesday? To the commercial, I mean?"

"Why?" I asked suspiciously.

"Well . . . I just thought that if you saw how dumb they were maybe you could tell Mom not to let me do any more of them."

Anyone could tell her how dumb they were just by turning on a TV set, so I didn't see how my opinion was going to change anything. But for some reason I felt kind of proud that Cam had asked me to come with him.

"Okay," I said.

"Thanks." Cam squirmed and wiggled and snorted his little "nyaw, nyaw" a few times. Then we both fell asleep, and we didn't wake up until morning.

When Cam came home without the cast later that afternoon, we decided to measure his arms. His right arm really was an inch shorter.

I'll be darned.

Two days later, we were in the car on the way to Cam's commercial. I glanced over my shoulder at him. He was sitting silently in the backseat, gazing out the rear window, and sucking his thumb. He hadn't done that since he was three years old! Should I let Mom know?

I was about to tell her. No, let the kid have his thumb, I decided. Brother! He was in worse shape than Max!

As Cam had predicted, the commercial turned out to be pretty bad. We got there ten minutes late, so Cam was whisked off to the makeup room before I could even wish him good luck.

Today the product was Wheat Tootles cereal (again!), and it looked like little trains or something. The cereal used to be shaped like horns, and this was a new gimmick for the commercial.

After about twenty minutes Cam took his place on the set, and a tall blonde woman told him what he was supposed to do. The set looked like someone's kitchen, except that it was cleaner than any kitchen I had ever been in. Cam had to wear an engineer's cap on his head, and he was holding a big train whistle. Actually, it looked more like a wooden harmonica, but it did sound like a train.

There was another kid in the commercial too—a little girl with red pigtails and a light blue dress. The ribbons on her pigtails matched her dress, and the bows on her shoes matched the ribbons.

Mom and I sat in the seats farthest away from the stage. I watched the cameraman scooting back and forth, and then a very short man with a black mustache signaled for all of us to be quiet.

"Wheat Tootles. TAKE ONE!" he shouted.

The girl with red pigtails began eating. Each time she took a spoonful of the cereal, Cam would blow the big train whistle right into her ear. The air passing through it made her blue satin ribbons vibrate. I guess Cam was supposed to be the pesty little brother—which made him perfect for the part, as far as I was concerned.

The little orange-haired girl, whose name was Brittany, shoveled the fifteenth spoonful of Wheat Tootles into her mouth. "It's going to be another neat, sweet, Wheat Tootles morning!" she said, turning her head to the right so that the camera angle could catch her cute little dimple.

"TOOT!" Cam blasted the whistle in her ear for the fifteenth time. Her ribbons flew for the fifteenth time.

"Hey, she's pretty good!" I whispered to Mom. "Still smiling, even with all that cereal in her gut."

"Hrmph!" snorted Mom. "I bet her hair is dyed."

"Shhhh!" The lady in front of us swiveled her

head around to glare at my mother. The woman's hair was even redder than Brittany's!

"Hers is dyed too," Mom said, after the woman faced the set again. I started to laugh. Mom frowned at me for a moment, but then she began to giggle too.

"Shhhh!" hissed Brittany's mother again, turning all the way around in her seat this time.

Mom and I stopped laughing.

What did that woman find so riveting about this boring commercial anyway? The fifteenth take looked just like the first one to me. Except that Cam seemed to be blowing the whistle a lot more during the later ones.

A tall, thin man came onto the set and suddenly started shouting something at the cameraman.

"Who's that?" I whispered to Mom.

Brittany's mom turned around to us again. "That's the producer," she said smugly.

The producer motioned to the short man with the mustache.

"That kid is too big!" he yelled, pointing a finger at Cam.

"He's small for his age!" piped in my mother. I felt like crawling under my seat. Maybe I could pretend that I was with Brittany's mother.

The tall man looked over his shoulder, squinting into the darkness. Jeez! I was sure glad that he couldn't see us!

"Who in the—" he began. His voice was drowned out by another blast of that irritating whistle. Why was Cam blowing that thing now? I winced and covered my ears. But my eyes were searching frantically for an emergency exit. Brittany's mother turned and scowled at us again.

Great, I thought to myself. If that man had been here from the beginning, he might have told Cam he was too big in the first place. Then I wouldn't have to be sitting here now, next to the crazy lady who yells at TV producers.

The filming was over at that point, and the producer told us that we could all go home. "And get rid of that blasted train whistle!" he shouted.

Someone handed it to Cam and said, "Here. Keep it, kid." Oh, wonderful!

All the way home Cam blew the whistle in my ear.

"TOOT!" His face went from hot pink to bright red. The sound was even worse than that snort he made in his sleep.

"Cut that out!" I screamed. "If you blow that thing in my ear one more time, I'll throw it out the window."

"You Mr. Potato Head!" Cam yelled back at me.

I pretended to be dying from his insult. "Oh—oh—hurt me some more," I teased.

"BOYS!" Mom held one arm over her forehead and draped the other across the top of the steering wheel. "If you want to get home alive, then stop yelling this instant. I mean it!"

I stared straight ahead out the window, and I guess Cam did the same. At least I didn't hear the train whistle again for a while.

Then I remembered my promise to Cam. I turned around to take a look at him. Too bad, buddy, I thought, but this is definitely not the best time to mention your retirement to Mom.

Chapter Eight

When we got back from the Wheat Tootles commercial, Mom was too upset to cook dinner. So she left Cam with me while she drove to the Shanghai Palace for some Chinese takeout food.

I sat down at my desk to finish my math homework. Thai was outside, and I could hear Cam laughing at some dumb TV show downstairs, so I decided it was probably safe to set Max down on the desk top and let him do a little exploring while I added fractions on my work sheet.

Since Max was too terrified to walk in his ball anymore, I wanted him to get some exercise so he wouldn't get fat. Of course, I had to keep an eye on him, just to make sure he didn't run away or hide somewhere.

Max sniffed the spine of my math book and

turned away, his nose twitching. Then he crawled all over my work sheet, finally stopping to lick his toes. I was so busy watching him that I didn't hear Cam until it was too late.

"TOOT!" Cam and his train whistle sprang up behind me, nearly ripping my eardrum out. Max was so frightened that he really let loose—and a huge yellow puddle began to spread all over my homework.

"That's it!" I screamed. "That thing has to go!" I yanked the whistle out of Cam's hand and heaved it out the window. Then I stared him down until his bottom lip started to quiver.

"I was just playin' around," he whimpered.

"Tell that to my teacher tomorrow," I said as I grabbed my math assignment and threw it on the bed. I picked Max up and rubbed his back gently, glaring at Cam. "I can't hand in my homework with pee all over it!"

Just then Mike walked into the room. And he was holding Cam's train whistle.

"Hey, what's going on?" he asked. "I was walking up the driveway and this thing came flying down—"

"Yaaaaaargh!" I screamed, making a lunge for it. But Cam grabbed the whistle from Mike first and sped out the door, down the hall, and locked himself in the bathroom. Mike and I chased after him, but the door slammed shut in front of our faces before we could grab him.

"You come out of there, Cam!" I shouted.

"TOOT!"

"Come out or I'll sit in this hallway here for eighty years!"

Silence.

"You'll grow old in that bathroom, Cam—and all you'll have to live on is Crest and Kaopectate."

There was still silence. A tiny worried feeling began to creep into my head, right behind the eyeballs. What was Cam doing in there anyway? Could a kid overdose on Flintstones vitamins?

Trying to stay calm, I carefully placed my ear right up against the door.

"Cam," I said quietly, "it's okay. I'm just outside the door. All you have to do is—"

"TOOT!" I jumped backward, slamming Mike against the wall as the noise blasted through my eardrum.

"How could you let him get it away from you?" I screamed at Mike.

"Get what away?" Mike yelled. "I don't even know what that thing IS!"

"It's a train whistle—which I tried to throw out the window before YOU got in the way!" I glared at him.

"Don't you look at me like that, Crane," Mike fumed. "I didn't ask to get mixed up in all this." Mike turned and huffed back to my bedroom. I just stared at the bathroom door, blinking slowly.

I was still clutching Max in my hand, and he was trembling slightly. Rubbing his back with one finger, I slowly followed Mike down the hall to return my hamster to his cage before he had another accident all over my fingers.

Mike was sitting stiffly on the edge of the bed. "I still don't see why you're so mad at me," he muttered.

"This is why," I answered, pointing at the damp work sheet lying on my bed.

"Peeee Uuuuuu. What's that?"

"That's what happened after Cam blew the train whistle at Max."

I could tell that Mike was trying not to laugh. "Where did Cam get the ear-blaster, anyway?" he asked.

"Oh, he got that from his TV commercial today," I explained to him, dumping my math work sheet in the wastebasket.

"Yeah? How did that go?"

"It was pretty dumb."

"So . . ." Mike began slowly, "you'll be playin' ball with Bobby Lorimer again, huh?" Then he grinned at me.

"What's so funny?" I asked.

"Well." Mike paused and sort of punched the bedspread down with his fist. "Don't you think she's kind of cute?"

CUTE!!! I couldn't believe it! I just gaped at him. Bobby Lorimer . . . cute? I had never really thought about it, to tell the truth. Most of the time she had too much bubble gum all over her face for me to tell.

"About as cute as a piranha," I answered finally.

"Yeah. Well. I was just wondering if you thought so," Mike said. I guess he knew now where I stood on that subject.

I glanced at the clock on my desk. Mom wasn't home yet, and I was getting pretty hungry. So Mike and I decided to go down to the kitchen and get some ice cream from the freezer.

As we started down the stairs, I thought I heard the bathroom door creak open, and I just knew we were being followed. I turned quickly and saw Cam disappear around the corner at the top of the stairs. At least he didn't have the train whistle with him.

"Copycat!" I yelled. "Stop following us!"

"I wasn't following you," Cam shouted. "I'm just going downstairs too."

Mike and I ignored him. Cam followed us, of course.

"I thought I told you to quit following us!" I said. Cam was now approaching stage three on the nuisance scale.

"Well . . . I need to go to the kitchen too."

"And I suppose you want some ice cream?"

"Yeah," he answered.

I snorted loudly and dug into the freezer.

"How's the TV biz?" Mike asked Cam.

"Oh. It's okay," Cam replied, sitting down heavily in an empty chair.

"Hard work, huh?"

"No."

It was pretty obvious to me that Cam didn't want to talk about the commercial, and I kind of wished Mike wouldn't ask him anything more about it.

Then Cam's face brightened a little. "The only good thing about it is the whistle they gave me," he said smugly. I slammed the bowl of ice cream down in front of him.

"Can I have some water too?" Cam demanded.

Brother! Just because he was on TV he thought he could slave me around. But I plunked down a glass of water for him too.

"Thanks, Les," he said. Then he gazed up at

me. "I'm sorry I followed you guys." Those eyes of his began to fill up with water. It must have been an instinct for survival, like the way certain animals use camouflage to keep from being eaten alive.

Poor kid. Cam probably just wanted some company. He didn't have any real friends, except for Jerome, and I think I scared him away for good after I found out that he and Cam had put Max into orbit.

"Where's your train whistle?" I asked, trying to be nice to him.

"I hid it. So you won't try to take it away from me again!" Cam stuck his tongue out at me. It was coated with vanilla ice cream.

"For crying out loud, Cam! I don't want your stupid whistle. Just keep it away from my eardrums from now on. Okay?"

My brother sniffed and took another bite of his ice cream. "Okay. Then can I play with you?"

I looked over at Mike, and he shrugged back at me.

So, after finishing my ice cream, I told Cam he could tag along. The three of us decided to go back upstairs and make Play-Doh hamsters for Max to play with. But when we got to the cage, we found the door wide open and no hamster in sight.

"Oh, no!" I groaned, plopping down on my bed and hugging a pillow to my stomach. "I forgot to latch the door when I put Max back inside." Now my hamster was loose, and Mom was due back any minute. And where was Thai, I suddenly wondered?

The three of us all stared at the empty cage, thinking the same thing. There was a Schizo Hamster—with an unpredictable bladder—hiding somewhere in this house!

Chapter Nine

As it turned out, my pee-stained homework didn't matter much, because the next morning I woke up with the chicken pox. At first, my mother was absolutely furious because I had exposed Cameron to it. I guess she was terrified that he would grow another three inches if he was out of commission for a few more weeks.

After she calmed down, though, Mom was really great. She brought me soup and ginger ale and comic books. And she even told Cam that he couldn't touch my slime men. But I think that might have been because she thought Cam would pick up some germs from them.

Never mind the fact that I was the one itching like crazy. Or that the final basketball tryouts were in just two and a half weeks and I probably wouldn't be able to practice for at least a week!

Cam stayed on his side of the room for the first few days. But curiosity eventually got the best of him.

"Can I see that big red spot on your stomach?" he asked me. "The one Mom told you to stop scratching?"

I eyed my brother carefully. "What's in it for me?"

Cam thought for a moment. Then he went over to the closet and pulled out his Monopoly game. He dumped his horde of Monopoly money on top of my bed and sat down to count each dollar bill.

"Here," he said, handing me a few bills. I guess he hadn't figured out yet that they wouldn't buy anything.

"This is a whole lot of money, huh, Les?" Cam asked. Then he started stacking the money in little piles by my feet.

"Hey, Cam?" I asked, wiggling my toes and toppling three of his piles. "How would you like to make some real money? Dime and quarter stuff?"

"Sure!" He stopped counting and jerked his head up to listen.

"I'm really worried about Max," I told him. "So there's something you can do for me, since I'm stuck here in bed. Set out food and water for Max—in places where Mom can't see it." Cam, Mike, and I had all agreed not to tell Mom about Max's disappearance. It would only make her jumpy. "Then you can check on the food later to see if he ate any of it. I don't want Max to starve, for Pete's sake."

"Why don't we just put some food in his cage and maybe he'll come back to it when he's hungry?"

You know, that was pretty smart thinking for a six-year-old. But I wasn't sure if it would really work.

"Yeah," I agreed. "You can make the cage one of your food stashes. That way, Mom won't get too suspicious."

"All right," Cam said, nodding slowly. "But how much do I get for it?"

"A dime a day."

Cam was thinking carefully about that. Dimes didn't seem as valuable as his paper money.

So I said, "A dime plus a Monopoly buck."

He still looked doubtful.

"And if I do get picked to go to basketball camp this summer, you can watch Max the whole time for me." Then I stopped and swallowed noisily. "If we FIND him, that is." Cam had been searching the house for me. He seemed really worried about my hamster too.

"You mean you want me to take care of Max?" Cam asked, eyeing me suspiciously. "For money?"

"Sure. I think you'd do a good job."

Well! You'd have thought I awarded him the Nobel Peace Prize or something. He was that proud. And for some reason, it made me feel good all over, even under my itchy chicken pox.

"Okay." Cam smiled at me.

Just then Mom came into our room with a strange look on her face—kind of like she didn't recognize me or something.

"There's a phone call for you, Les," she said. Then she stared real hard at me. "It's a girl."

Cam started giggling. I crawled out of bed and stumbled down the hall, scratching my arm.

"Hello," I said. I felt a little dizzy now that I was on two feet.

"Hi, Ichabod! It's Bobby Lorimer."

Oh, jeez! What did SHE want?

"I was wondering if you'd like to shoot a few baskets this afternoon," she continued.

"NO!" I said. "I mean, I can't. I have the chicken pox."

"The what!" Then I heard her laughing loudly

on the other end. "You're supposed to get that in first or second grade!"

"Thanks for the sympathy."

"Mmmmm. Sorry."

There was a long silence, except for the sound of her chewing gum. I considered hanging up.

"Maybe I'll stop by and visit you sometime then. When you're feeling better," she suggested. "How about next week?"

"Okay," I mumbled. I just wanted to get back into bed.

"Where do you live?"

I must have been very light-headed, because I actually gave her my address. After she hung up, I wondered how she had gotten my phone number.

I managed to find my way back to the bedroom, and I crawled under the covers, shivering.

"Who was that?" my mom asked. Had she been listening the whole time?

"A girl from the basketball tryouts."

"A girl was trying out?" Mom sat on the bed and rubbed my back through the covers. It felt really good.

"Yeah. And she made it to the finals too."

My mother was silent for a few moments, but she kept rubbing my back. "What did this girl want?" she asked me.

"To shoot some baskets."

Then my mom did something I didn't understand at all. She started to cry. I was just lying in
bed, listening to her blubber, and my chicken
pox itched like crazy!

"I'm sorry, Les," Mom finally said. "It's just
that you're growing up so fast. Girls are already
calling you on the telephone."

"A girl, Mom. Not girls."

She pooh-poohed that with a wave of her arm.
"Next thing I know, you'll be SHAVING!" she
cried, her eyes starting to water up again.

"Come on, Mom! I'm only eleven years old!"

Cam walked in just then with his bag of hamster munchies. When he saw Mom, he quickly hid
the sack behind his back.

"What do you have there?" Mom asked him.

"Nothing. It's nothing."

She eyed him warily but decided to let it rest.
With a big sigh, she stood up and patted my back
again.

"Just let me know when you need that razor,
Les," she said. Then she turned and left the
room.

"Razor?" Cam asked, looking puzzled.

"Never mind. Let's see what you have in
there."

Cam emptied out the contents of the bag, and

we discussed possible hiding places for the food. Max could be hiding out anywhere in the house, and I wanted to make sure that wherever he was, he would eventually run into something to eat.

After seven days of lying around in bed, I was finally pronounced not contagious anymore. I was still pretty weak, though, and could only practice shooting hoops with Mike a couple of afternoons.

My hamster had been missing the whole time. Cam and I were both hiding food for him, and some of the food had been eaten—so he was probably safe. But where was he hiding? I was really worried about him. It was just a matter of time before Thai found Max—or Mom found the food!

"Do you think Max could be in the wall someplace?" I asked Cam, tapping at a space beside the refrigerator.

"Maybe," said Cam. He reached his arm up too, but I grabbed it, studying the three tiny bumps near his wrist.

"Here's something else you'd better hide from Mom," I said.

"Huh?"

"Chicken pox!"

Chapter Ten

By the time I really recovered enough to play a good game of one-on-one with Mike, Cam was in bed and couldn't bother us.

Our cat had taken to wandering around the house in a state of confusion, wondering what had happened to his tormentor. Without Cam pouncing on him every day, I think Thai had misplaced a part of his identity. He would bump into furniture, clinging to table legs. And the slightest noise would send him straight up the dining room curtains. I hoped that he was so worried about Cam he wouldn't know what to do with Max if he did find him.

The final tryouts were only one day away, and Mike and I were running through some passing and lay-up drills in my driveway. I was very nervous, especially since I hadn't gotten much practicing in the last two weeks. Just as I was starting to run for an easy lay-up shot, Mom gunned her car into the driveway, leaning on the horn. "Hey!" I yelled, leaping sideways and knocking Mike over onto the grass.

"I'm sorry, Les," Mom said hurriedly, as she stepped out of the car and slammed the door behind her. "I've just had some very disturbing news. Oh, hi, Mike." She charged into the house, and I helped Mike back up to his feet.

"Terror on Wheels," he said, and we both cracked up. Sometimes it's good to laugh about stuff when you're really nervous.

I took a few more shots and then passed off to Mike. But he was just standing there in the middle of the driveway, with his mouth hanging open, staring over my right shoulder. I turned around in time to see Bobby Lorimer wheel her bicycle up to me and slam on her brakes. Terror on Wheels II, I thought.

"Hi, Ichabod!" she said, swinging one leg over her bike and tapping down the kickstand. "Sorry I didn't get over here until now. I guess you're just about over the chicken pox, huh?" She leaned forward and stood up on her tiptoes to get a better look at my face.

"Uh . . . yeah," I muttered. The smell of strawberry bubble gum stuck in my nose and began working its way down into my throat.

"Well, I just came by to wish you good luck in the tryouts tomorrow." She seemed to hesitate when she saw Mike hovering behind me.

Then Mike began dribbling the basketball noisily and whistling. He took a couple of shots and then dribbled some more, totally ignoring Bobby and me.

"Ummm . . . thanks," I said to Bobby. I could see that I was not going to win any prizes today for stimulating dialogue.

Bobby looked at Mike and then back at me with a little shrug.

"Well, see ya!" she shouted. Then she hopped back on her bike and pedaled around the corner.

I glanced over my shoulder at Mike. He had stopped dribbling the ball now, and he had this goofy smile on his face. It made me sick. Did he still believe that I thought Bobby was cute?

"What did Bobby mean . . . she didn't get over here until now?" Mike asked me. Then he tossed me the ball, and I dribbled it a few times.

"Nothing," I answered very quickly.

"How did she know where you live?"

"I told her."

"You what?" Mike started laughing again, so I had to set him straight.

"She called me when I was sick."

"Oh, man! Oooh-weee! You've got it bad!" howled Mike, clutching his stomach.

"Me! It was you who said Bobby Lorimer was cute!"

"But she wasn't calling ME on the telephone!" he hooted. Mike must have enjoyed laughing alone, because I didn't think this was funny at all.

Luckily, Cam poked his head out the bedroom window just then and yelled down to me. "Hey, Les? Can you come up here?"

I looked at Mike and shrugged. He started to leave and then turned around at the end of the driveway.

"Good luck tomorrow!" he shouted, throwing an imaginary punch with his fist.

"Thanks!" I answered. Then I had to chuckle a little. The look on Mike's face when Bobby Lorimer pedaled up my driveway had been pretty funny.

As I entered my room, I saw Cam propped up in bed, looking very happy with himself.

"You look like you just found Max," I said. Then I glanced over to see if maybe my hamster had returned. The cage was still empty.

"Nooooo," Cam replied, grinning at me. "This is even better. Mom said I don't have to be on TV anymore." Then he paused. "Maybe."

I was very surprised. I sat down on my own bed and started to untie the laces on my high tops.

"How come?" I asked, kicking the shoes off.

"They told Mom that I'm getting too big."

"Who told Mom?"

"The people at the ad agency. I bet the Wheat Tootles people told them."

"Yeah. Well. You are getting too big."

"I know." Then Cam paused to scratch. "But they told her something else."

"What?" I leaned forward with my elbows on my knees.

"That I'm *un . . . un*"— he stopped to think— *opative.*"

"Unoperative? You mean like you're broken and need to get fixed?"

"No! No! I don't . . . um . . . CO-operate."

"Oh. You mean you're uncooperative." This was no news to me.

"Yeah. That's what Mom said they said."

"Hmmmm. Why did they tell her that?"

"Well, I blew the whistle right in the producer's ear. On purpose."

I suddenly remembered that afternoon at the studio. No wonder Cam kept blowing that thing so many times!

"You mean like when he was trying to talk?" I asked.

"Yeah."

Well, I'll be darned. The kid did have guts. He hadn't just tried to get Mom angry. He went for the producer of the whole commercial!

"So they're doing the commercial again. With a smaller kid in it," Cam added. "Someone who doesn't blow so hard."

"How did Mom take that?" I asked him.

"Oooooh. She was so mad. But then I told her I hated it."

"What did she do then?"

"She cried."

"You should have told her before, Cam. She might have listened."

"Yeah . . . I know."

"Don't you like being on TV at all?" I asked him. "Even a little?"

Cam just shrugged. "Nah," he said. "The lights make me hot. And the makeup smells funny. I just want to play with Jerome. And I want you to teach me how to play basketball." He punched his pillow and started scratching again.

I walked over to Cam's bed and sat down next to him. "Okay. I can give you some pointers," I said, patting him awkwardly on the back.

Cam looked up at me and smiled. "Jerome too?"

"Jerome too."

Maybe Cam just wasn't old enough to really enjoy fame yet.

During dinner Dad had a few words to say to Cam about the possible end of his career. "Now, let me get this straight," Dad began. "You purposely blew that whistle at times when it was inappropriate?"

"Yes." Cam stirred his mashed potatoes around in the middle of his plate.

"So you not only wasted their time, but your time and your mother's as well?"

"Yes." The stirring stopped. Cam's hands were now in his lap.

"And you probably caused your mother some embarrassment."

"He certainly did," my mom interrupted, her face bright red. It probably was embarrassing to have a complete stranger tell you that your kid is totally out of control.

My mom and dad both wore their serious look, and I think Cam was beginning to realize that just explaining his feelings to Mom might have been the easy way out, after all.

"What do you think would be a good trade-off for your behavior?" Dad asked quietly. He always did that to us—made us choose our own form of torture.

"No TV tonight?" Cam suggested.

"That's good for starters."

"No dessert either?"

Dad looked at Mom, and she nodded.

"And you're grounded for a week," she added. I thought that was pretty funny, considering that Cam had the chicken pox anyway.

"Okay," Dad said. Then his face sort of re-formed itself into a sad smile. "I'm sorry you were so miserable, Cam."

"We really had no idea," Mom added quickly. And I was sure she didn't.

But that didn't stop her from trying again. "There are still two more agencies who need older children—" Mom stopped and looked at the three of us. She folded her hands on top of the table.

Then she said slowly, "I won't call them now if you don't want me to, Cam. But let's discuss it in a few weeks, okay?"

"Okay," Cam answered. "May I be excused now?"

"Sure, son," Dad said.

"Me too?" I asked.

"You too." Then Dad held out his hand across the table. "Good luck tomorrow, Les. We'll be rooting for you."

The tryouts! The day I had been hoping for and dreading was tomorrow! All those hours of practice could pay off. Or they could fly out the window in just a few hours. I mean, I knew I was good. But was I good enough?

Suddenly a big lump formed in my throat. "Thanks," I replied. And I shook my dad's hand back.

After watching TV for a half hour, I decided to go to bed early so that I would be ready for the tryouts tomorrow. But as I was putting on my pajamas, I noticed a half-empty bowl of melting ice cream sitting in the middle of Cam's bed, near his knees. My brother was already curled up under the covers, pretending to be asleep.

"What's that?" I demanded, picking up the bowl and waving it in front of his nose.

"Nothing. I was just looking at it."

I looked at the ice cream with him. There wasn't much left to see in there. "You were watching it melt?"

I sat down on the bed next to Cam and pulled down the covers. Then I pointed to his hand, which was hidden under the pillow.

"What do you have under there?" I asked.

Cam shrugged and pulled out a spoon. "But I wasn't going to eat it all," he protested quickly. "I was just looking at it."

I really couldn't help it. I started to laugh.

"Don't tell on me," Cam pleaded. "Or else I'll tell Mom and Dad about that girl you and Mike were talking to this afternoon."

The last thing I wanted was for Mom to start crying about girls and shaving again. It was too embarrassing! So I handed over the ice cream.

Cam dipped the spoon into the bowl and started eating. Then he stopped.

"Want a bite?"

"Sure." I took the spoon and we finished off the ice cream together.

Of course, Mom gave in and carried up a tray of milk and cookies for Cam around 8:30. She didn't even say a word about the sticky bowl on the floor.

After she left, we turned out the light and I tried to get some sleep. I rolled over onto my stomach and concentrated on the shots I would use in the game tomorrow. This was not the best thing to do, since what I really needed for tomorrow was a good night's sleep.

Suddenly Cam started to giggle.

"Be quiet!" I hissed at him.

He giggled again.

"What's so funny?" I finally asked.

"When I jiggle my stomach up and down, I can hear the milk sloshing around in there. You wanna listen?"

Oh, brother! The night before the biggest day in my life and I had to share it with a snorting milk slosher!

Chapter Eleven

The sun slanting across my face woke me in the morning. I rolled out of bed and immediately tripped over Cam's empty ice cream bowl. Then I bumped into Max's cage, and noticed that all the food was missing from his dish inside. That meant my hamster must have been here last night!

Max was alive! And he was hungry, which must be a good sign. Maybe it was an omen that I would make the team this afternoon. I quietly went downstairs and fixed myself a bowl of cereal.

Dad shuffled in with the morning paper and nodded at me.

"Nervous?" he asked.

"Petrified."

"Just relax," Dad advised me. "Remember, they're not timing you out there. Ten shots made out of ten shots tried looks better than ten out of thirty." I thought about that. He was right. I should take my time and go for the shots I knew I could make. If I was covered, it was better to pass off to some other guy who was open for a much better shot. Dad should have been a coach. No, on second thought, Dad should have been a team manager. Mom should have been a coach.

Even though Dad offered to take me to the county gym, I decided to ride my bike instead. The exercise would help to loosen my legs—and calm my nerves.

Downstairs in the locker room I changed into a faded blue tank top and white shorts. When I got inside the gym, I noticed that these courts were much bigger than the ones we had played on three weeks ago. And a lot shinier too.

One of the referees handed me a paper bib with the number 72 on it. I pinned it onto the front of my shirt, but my fingers shook so much that it took three times before I could get the number on straight. I'd never seen so many tall kids in one place before. They were all practicing their shots, and basketballs were flying every which way through the room. I could hear the steady rhythm of balls bouncing and sneakers squeaking across the floor.

I wandered over to one of the courts, keeping an eye out for anyone I knew. Tim and Bobby Lorimer were at the top of the key, taking practice throws.

"Hi," I said, trying to sound casual.

"Hi, Ichabod," Bobby answered. I winced and glanced over at Tim. He just put out his hands and gave me the high five.

"Free throws are not Bobby's strong point," Tim said with a grin.

Bobby started to say something, then changed her mind, angrily blowing a big round bubble instead. She was chewing on a wad of gum that must have been the size of my fist.

"Relax," I told her. "They're not timing you out there. Ten shots made out of ten shots tried looks better than ten out of thirty."

Bobby seemed impressed.

"Yeah," added Tim. "That means you pass the ball to Les or me whenever you get the chance!" We both laughed, but Bobby just glared at us.

"And you know, Bobby," I continued, "if you spit out the gum, your shots'll be better."

"Fat chance, pencil neck!" she snapped, jutting

her tiny chin out and chomping harder than ever. I guess I had sort of overstepped my boundaries, but I really was only trying to help her.

A man in a green baseball cap walked into the center of the gym and blew on his whistle—three short blasts. This was it! I felt like my knees were going to take off in two opposite directions.

This time we were using all four courts. The players would rotate to a different position on a new court every ten minutes. That way, the judges could see how we played on both offense and defense. They could also watch how we performed against different opponents.

Luckily, Bobby and I started off on separate courts. It was much easier for me to concentrate on working the ball in for a better shot when I didn't have to worry about tripping all over her. We switched around after ten minutes, though, and I did have to play on the same team with Bobby for a while.

She was good! For someone so small, she was very aggressive, and she also turned out to be an excellent ball hawker. One guy on the other team kept trying to close in on me, but Bobby really had him covered. He couldn't come near me as long as she was guarding him.

With Bobby on my man, I decided to take my

chance. I made a basic cut movement to the right and went for an outside shot. The ball shimmied in the hoop for a few horrifying seconds, but then it fell through the net.

"Good shot, Leslie!" Bobby yelled, but I was pumped up from the game and I didn't realize what she had called me.

When the final whistle blew, I was so exhausted that I didn't even care whether I made the final pick or not. If camp was going to be this hard, I probably wouldn't survive the first week anyway.

I walked slowly to the lower bleachers, plopping myself down and wiping a sweaty arm across my eyebrows.

Bobby charged over and sat next to me. I didn't really mind, though. At least she was someone to talk to. I noticed that she wasn't chewing gum either.

"Where's Tim?" I asked her.

"Oh, he's chatting it up with his buddies from last year." She held her nose up in the air and then shrugged as if it didn't bother her to be left out. But I knew it did. Tim must have been her idol or something.

Then I thought about Cam and how he broke his arm trying to be like me. I figured that little sisters were about as weird as little brothers. Probably weirder.

"Do you think we'll be picked?" Bobby asked. She was staring up at me, and it made me feel funny. Like maybe she really thought my opinion was worth a hoot or something. I stopped to think about it: Could two fifth-grade nobodies really be chosen out of a group of forty kids, when there were only eight spots available? No. It was impossible.

"Sure," I told her confidently, blowing out a big breath of air. Some local TV station was setting up cameras on the other side of the gym. I hadn't realized this was such big news.

Just then the judges signaled all of us to gather around. Bobby reached into her pocket and pulled out some gum. I had never seen anyone unwrap and start to chew a piece of bubble gum so fast in my entire life. It was like one continuous motion—a flick of the wrist.

"This is it!" she screamed, grabbing my hand. I yanked it back and shoved both of my hands into my pockets. But for some reason, my fingertips were tingling.

That big guy in the green cap was announcing the winners. What a job! Making or breaking some poor kid's day. He was explaining that only five players would actually be chosen for the final team. But there would also be three alternates, and all eight kids could attend the camp. Then he started right off announcing the winners in our category.

After about three names were called in our age group, I gave up hope. All those guys he named were much stronger ballplayers than I was, and I knew it. Then I heard him shout out the name of the last winner: "Tim Lorimer."

Tim! He made it! At least I was glad for him.

Next came the alternates. First: a name I didn't recognize. Second: Robinette Lorimer. Bobby? My heart felt like it had sunk down into my stomach and was stuck there. Bobby had beaten me.

I guess I was so set to lose that I didn't even hear the guy say my name. All I knew was that suddenly Bobby was hugging me and shouting, "We made it, Ichabod! We made it!"

I just let myself smile real slow. I didn't hug Bobby back, but I didn't exactly stop her either.

All of a sudden some bright lights were shining directly into my eyes. For a few seconds I couldn't see anything. But I heard plenty.

"Well, little lady," exclaimed a female voice I recognized from the Channel 11 news, "how does it feel to be the only girl chosen to attend the county basketball camp this summer?"

"Ummmm. It's neat. I guess," I heard Bobby

stammer. I probably couldn't have done much better, under the circumstances.

"And here she is, ladies and gentlemen," the woman reporter droned on, "right here from our own town of Riverdale: little Leslie Crane."

Bobby started giggling, and I groaned loudly. It was the old baby-picture curse again.

"I'm not Leslie Crane!" Bobby shouted into the microphone. "HE is. And we are the only two fifth graders who made the team!" Then Bobby grabbed my arm and shoved me out in front of her.

I blinked into the lights a few times, but I didn't hear anything else the reporter had to say. I was too busy being mortified. It must have been my fate in life to be constantly mistaken for a girl—only this time it would probably appear on the TV news.

Chapter Twelve

Although it was a little out of my way, I decided to stop by Mike's house on the way home. He was the one person I really wanted to talk to about the tryouts. And I knew he'd ask for a description of every play.

Little bits and pieces of the games kept popping back into my memory, like the great rim shot I made and the way Bobby had shouted at me. I pedaled faster and faster, reliving every glorious moment—except for the lady reporter from Channel 11.

I figured that Mike might be jealous, but when I told him that I was one of the team alternates, he jumped up and down, hooting and hollering. Then he punched me in the arm. People don't find friends like Mike very often.

"Did Bobby make the team too?" he prodded me.

"Yeah," I answered slowly.

"Oooooh." Then Mike began to chant, "Bobby and Leslie, sitting in a tree, *K-I-S—*"

"Just lay off," I shouted, but I grinned at him anyway. I felt too great right now to let one single thing bother me.

We rode back to my house together, and Mike offered to send postcards of Riverdale to me at sports camp, just in case I was crazy enough to even THINK about getting homesick. He said one look at those would cure me for sure!

As we stepped into the house, I was ready to make my grand entrance, but all we could hear were Mom's hysterical screeches from the kitchen. Where was everyone else? Some moment of glory this had turned out to be.

Mike and I headed toward the kitchen to investigate, and Thai dashed by so fast that he crashed into one of the legs of our dining room table.

"Cam is after him again," I informed Mike.

But Cam was not in the kitchen. Only my mother was there, squatting on the floor next to the refrigerator, and her head was bent down low over something.

"Sorry, guys," she said when she heard us

enter, but she didn't lift her head. "I thought Thai had a rat in his mouth, and when I screamed he dropped it and ran." Then Mom looked up at me. "I hate to tell you this, Les, but I think it's—"

"Max!" I hollered, nearly knocking her over to get a good look at him.

There was my poor neurotic hamster, a small brown lump lying beside Mom's knee. I picked him up and cradled him in one palm.

My mother pressed her lips together and frowned. "Is he ummmmm . . . you know?"

"Dead?" Mike blurted out.

"No. I think he just fainted," I replied, feeling a tiny up-and-down movement in my hand, which I took to mean that Max was breathing.

"Fainted?" Mom asked, lifting her eyebrows at me.

"You don't know Max, Mom."

She stood up and brushed a strand of hair out of her eyes. "Oh, Les! I forgot to tell you. I saw you on TV this afternoon! I'm so proud of you, I could just burst!" She squeezed me and Max up to her chest.

TV! Did she mean what I thought she meant?

"WHAT?" Mike shrieked. He turned to me. "Why didn't you tell me?"

Was I ever glad he didn't watch the news.

"Oh, I didn't think you'd be interested," I answered, trying to look bored.

"That's all right, Mike," Mom chimed in. "I videotaped it!"

First Cam on video. Now me.

As Mom charged off to find the videotape, Dad and Cam burst into the kitchen with a huge pizza in a box. Cam still had some pox marks on his face, but he looked a whole lot better than he had a few days ago.

"This is to celebrate!" my dad yelled. "I took the afternoon off!" Then he gave me a big hug. "We're so proud of you, son."

"Let's watch the videotape!" shouted Mike. I should have warned him about the interview earlier, but now it was too late.

We all took seats in the den, munching on pizza, while Mom fiddled with the video recorder.

Suddenly there was Bobby on our TV, talking to the reporter. The pizza in my stomach turned into a pepperoni bowling ball.

Then I watched as Bobby said, "I'm not Leslie Crane. HE is! And we are the only two fifth graders who made the team!"

The camera backed up, and she shoved me right in front of her. I must have blinked twenty

102

times in that one minute. I looked like one of those pod people whose minds were taken over by the body snatchers.

And now I just sat straight up on the couch, waiting for the sound of hysterical laughter. But no one was laughing.

"Hooray!" yelled Mike, waving his pizza slice in the air over his head. "It's Leslie Crane: THE STAR!"

"Let's watch it again!" shouted Cam. Then he blew on his train whistle. Cam seemed to enjoy watching me on TV, but maybe that was just because Mom had finally let him get out of bed. And I did notice that he was blowing that horn loudest whenever anyone started to say something great about me.

Mom laughed and rewound the tape. We watched it again. And again. And again. I was floating on air. Leslie Crane: THE STAR.

The phone rang and Mom ran to answer it. When she rushed back into the den, she was beaming at me.

"It's for you," she exclaimed. "And it's Bobby Lorimer."

Mike and Cam whistled and hooted, but I didn't care. Nothing could ever ruin this day. Max was alive, and I was on the team.

As I left the room, I heard Mom say, "She's such a cute little girl."

Then Cam asked, "Is Les in love with Bobby Lorimer?"

Oh, jeez!

I picked up the phone in the hall and heard Bobby's voice.

"Hey, Ichabod! We were on TV!"

"I know. I saw."

"Wasn't it HOT? My parents even got it on videotape."

"Mine too."

"Well—uh—congratulations."

"Hey—you too!"

She sort of giggled a little. "I guess I'll see you at camp then."

"Yeah. I guess so."

Silence.

"Well . . . bye, Bobby."

"Bye, Leslie."

I hung up and started to make my way back to the den. But then I stopped. She had called me Leslie. And I guess it didn't sound that bad. I thought about when I was standing behind her and those hot television lights were making my forehead sweat. All I could smell was that strawberry bubble gum, and it made me feel light all

104

over. Sort of like my brain was in a gray, fuzzy numbness. And I found that I liked the feeling.

Maybe spending three weeks at basketball camp with a girl wouldn't be so horrible, after all.

But then, that's another story.

About the Author

Alison Jackson grew up in Pasadena, California. She graduated from the University of California at Irvine and San Jose State University. She lives in Huntington Beach, California, with her husband and two children. While working as a librarian she observed a class about getting children started in commercials. This inspired her to write *My Brother the Star* (available from Minstrel Books). Her next story about Leslie Crane is *Crane's Rebound,* coming from Minstrel Books in the spring of 1993.